This edition published in 1993 by Mimosa Books,
distributed by Outlet Book Company, Inc., a Random House Company,
40 Engelhard Avenue, Avenel, New Jersey 07001.

2 4 6 8 10 9 7 5 3 1

First published in 1993 by Grisewood & Dempsey Ltd.
Copyright © Grisewood & Dempsey Ltd. 1981, 1991, 1993

ISBN 1 85698 501 6

Printed and bound in Italy

RAPUNZEL
AND OTHER STORIES

MIMOSA
·**BOOKS**·

NEW YORK • AVENEL, NEW JERSEY

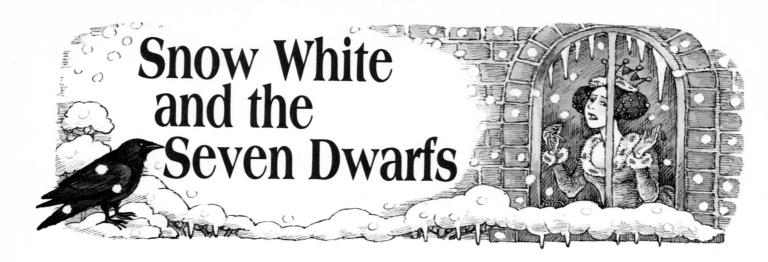

Snow White and the Seven Dwarfs

One winter a beautiful queen sat sewing by a window. As she gazed down at the snow-covered garden she saw a black raven and, at the same moment, she happened to prick her finger on her needle – a drop of blood fell on the snow. The colors were so strong that the queen said to herself, "If only I could have a child whose skin was as white as snow, with hair as black as a raven, and lips as red as blood."

Not long afterward the queen had a baby daughter, and when she saw her jet black hair, snowy white skin, and red lips she rememberd her strange wish on that winter's day and named her Snow White.

But after a few years Snow White's mother died and her father married again. The new queen, Snow White's stepmother, was beautiful too, but she was also proud and vain. She had a magic mirror and each day she would admire herself in it and ask,

'Mirror, mirror, on the wall,
Who is the fairest one of all?"
and the mirror would always reply,
"You, O Queen, are the fairest one of all."
The queen would smile when she heard this for she knew the

mirror always spoke the truth. As the years went by, Snow White grew prettier and prettier, until one day, when the queen looked in the magic mirror, the mirror replied,

"You, O Queen, are fair, 'tis true,

But Snow White is fairer now than you."

The queen was filled with envy. From that day on she hated Snow White. Finally she called for a hunter and told him to take Snow White deep into the forest and kill her.

"Cut out her heart and bring it back to me to prove she is dead," she commanded.

The hunter felt very sad. Like everyone in the king's household he loved Snow White, but he knew he must obey the queen's orders. He took Snow White deep into the forest and pulled out his knife. Snow White fell to her knees in terror. The hunter took pity on her and told her to hide. Then he killed a deer and cut out its heart to take back to the cruel queen.

On her own in the forest, Snow White felt afraid. She began to run here and there through the trees, but she did not know which way to go. In the evening she came to a clearing and found a little house. She wondered if it was a woodman's cottage where she might be able to stay. When she knocked at the door, there was no answer.

Snow White lifted the latch and went inside. There she saw a room all neat and tidy with a little table laid with seven places — seven little knives and forks, seven little wooden plates and drinking cups. Snow White was hungry and thirsty so she ate some food from each plate and drank a drop from each cup. She did not want to empty one person's plate and cup only.

Beyond the table were seven little beds all neatly made. Snow White tried them all out and the seventh bed was just right. She lay down and fell into a deep sleep, exhausted by her long journey through the forest.

The cottage was the home of seven dwarfs. All day long they worked in a mine nearby, digging diamonds from deep inside the mountain. When they returned home that night, they were startled to see that someone had entered their cottage and had taken some food and drink from each place at their table. They were even more surprised to find their beds disturbed. When the seventh dwarf found Snow White in his bed he called to the others. They all gathered around her and marveled at her beauty. Being kind little men they decided not to disturb her.

When Snow White awoke the next day she told the dwarfs her story. "I have no home now," she said sadly, and at once the dwarfs asked her to stay with them in the cottage. Snow White agreed happily, and each morning when the dwarfs went off to work, she stayed behind and kept their cottage clean and cooked their supper.

At the palace the queen welcomed the hunter when he returned with the deer's heart. She was certain that once again she was the most beautiful woman in the world. As soon as she was alone she looked in her magic mirror and said,

"Mirror, mirror, on the wall,
Who is the fairest one of all?"

To her horror, the mirror replied,

"You, O Queen, are fair, 'tis true,
But Snow White is fairer still than you."

The queen trembled with rage as she realized that the hunter had tricked her. She decided that she would seek out Snow White and kill her herself.

The queen disguised herself as an old pedlar woman with a tray of ribbons and pretty things to sell and she set off into the forest. When she came to the dwarfs' cottage she knocked and cried out, "Pretty goods for sale! Pretty goods for sale!"

Snow White came to the door and looked eagerly at the tray. The queen noticed that she was attracted by some lacing ribbons and asked if Snow White would like to try one on. Snow White nodded, so the queen threaded a ribbon through her bodice. Then she tugged the lacing so tight that Snow White could not breathe and fell to the ground. The queen hurried back to the palace sure that this time Snow White was truly dead.

When the dwarfs returned that evening, they found Snow White lying on the floor, deathly cold and still. They gathered around her in dismay. Then they noticed that she had a new lacing on her dress which had been tied too tightly. Quickly they cut it open and Snow White started breathing again.

All seven dwarfs gave a tremendous sigh of relief as by now they loved Snow White dearly. She told them what had happened. The dwarfs suspected that the old pedlar woman was Snow White's wicked stepmother and that she would try to harm Snow White again if she ever found out that she was still alive. They begged her not to allow anyone into the cottage while she was alone and told her not to buy anything from strangers.

At the palace the queen smiled at her reflection in the magic mirror and asked,

> "Mirror, mirror, on the wall,
> Who is the fairest one of all?"

and the mirror replied,

> "You, O Queen, are fair,
> 'tis true,
> But Snow White is fairer
> still than you."

The queen was speechless with rage. She realized that yet again her plan to kill Snow White had failed. She resolved to try again and this time she was determined to succeed. She chose an apple with one rosy-red side and one yellow side. Carefully she injected poison into the red part of the apple and carefully she placed it in a basket of apples, on the very top.

The wicked queen, disguised this time as a peasant woman, set out once more into the forest. Once more she knocked at the dwarfs' cottage. She knew that Snow White would be wary by now so she simply chatted to her and, as Snow White became less nervous, she offered her an apple as a present. Snow White was tempted as the rosy apple looked delicious but she refused, explaining that she had been told not to accept anything from strangers.

"I will show you how harmless it is," said the disguised queen. "I will take a bite first and if I am unharmed you will know that it is safe." The queen had not poisoned the yellow side of the apple so she took a bite from there. When nothing happened, Snow White stretched out her hand for the apple. She too took a bite, but from the rosey-red side. Instantly the poison attacked Snow White and she fell down as though dead. The triumphant queen cackled with glee as she returned to the palace.

When the dwarfs found Snow White that evening they could not revive her. All night they watched over her, but when morning came and still she did not move or speak, they decided she must be dead.

Weeping bitterly, the dwarfs laid her in a coffin and placed a glass lid over the top so that all could admire her beauty even though she was dead. Then they carried the coffin to the top of a hill where night and day they stood guard over their beautiful Snow White.

The wicked queen was delighted that day when she looked in her mirror and asked,

"Mirror, mirror, on the wall,
who is the fairest one of all?"

and the mirror replied,

"You, O Queen, are the fairest one of all."

She gave a cruel laugh when she heard those words. They meant that her plan to kill Snow White had at last succeeded.

As the years passed, the story of Snow White's beauty spread far and wide. One day a prince came to see the coffin for himself. Snow White looked so lovely that he fell in love with her at once and asked the dwarfs to allow him to take the coffin with him back to his own country. The dwarfs loved Snow White too much to permit him to do this, but they agreed to let him kiss her.

As the prince gently raised Snow White's head to kiss her, the piece of poisoned apple fell from her lips and she stirred a little. She

12

was alive.

"Where am I?" she asked, looking at the prince.

"Safe with me," replied the prince, and Snow White too fell in love.

At that moment, the wicked queen was looking in her mirror and the mirror said,

"You, O Queen, are fair 'tis true,

But Snow White is fairer still than you."

The queen cursed Snow White in fury. But by now the king had discovered what evil deeds the queen had planned and he banished her from his kingdom. That night she left the palace and no one ever saw her or her mirror again.

Snow White said farewell to her kind friends, the seven dwarfs, and rode away with her prince. They were married at his father's castle and lived for a long time afterward in happiness and peace.

The Gingerbread Man

An old woman was baking one day, and she made some gingerbread. She had some dough left over, so she made the shape of a little man. She made eyes for him, a nose and a smiling mouth all of currants, and put currants down his front to look like buttons. Then she laid him on a baking tray and put him in the oven.

After a little while, she heard something rattling at the oven door. She opened it and to her surprise out jumped the little gingerbread man. She tried to catch him, but he slipped past her, calling as he ran.

"Run, run, as fast as you can,
You can't catch me, I'm the gingerbread man!"

She chased after him into the garden where her husband was digging. He put down his spade and tried to catch him too, but the

gingerbread man ran past him, calling,

"Run, run, as fast as you can,
You can't catch me, I'm the gingerbread man!"

He ran down the road with the old woman and the old man following. Soon he passed a cow. The cow called out, "Stop, gingerbread man! You look good enough to eat!" But the gingerbread man laughed and shouted over his shoulder,

"I've run from an old woman
And an old man.
Run, run, as fast as you can,
You can't catch me, I'm the gingerbread man!"

He ran on with the old woman and the old man and the cow following, and soon they all passed a horse. "Stop!" called the horse. "I'd like to eat you." But the gingerbread man called out,

"I've run from an old woman
And and old man.
And a cow!
Run, run, as fast as you can,
You can't catch me,
I'm the gingerbread man!"

He ran on, with the old woman and the old man and the cow and the horse following, and soon they passed some people making hay. "Stop!" they shouted. "You look good enough to eat." But the gingerbread man called out,

"I've run from an old woman
And from an old man.
And a cow and a horse!
Run, run, as fast as you can,
You can't catch me,
I'm the gingerbread man!"

He ran across the fields with the old woman and the old man, the cow and the horse and the haymakers all following. Soon he met a fox and called out,

"Run, run, as fast as you can,
You can't catch me,
I'm the gingerbread man!"

The sly fox thought to himself, "That gingerbread man looks good enough to eat," but he said nothing. He waited until the gingerbread man reached a wide deep swift-flowing river, with the old woman and the old man, the cow and the horse and the haymakers all chasing after him. Now the sly fox said,

"Jump on my back, Gingerbread Man, and I'll take you across the river!"

The gingerbread man jumped on the fox's back and the fox began to swim. As they reached the middle of the river, where the water was deep, the fox said,

"Stand on my head, Gingerbread Man, or you will get wet."

So the gingerbread man stood on the fox's head. As the current flowed more swiftly, the fox said,

"Move onto my nose, Gingerbread Man, so that I can carry you more safely. I would not like you to drown."

The gingerbread man slid onto the fox's nose. But when they reached the bank on the far side of the river, the fox suddenly went SNAP! The gingerbread man disappeared into the fox's mouth and was never seen or heard of again.

The Great Big Turnip

Once upon a time, in Russia, an old man planted some turnip seeds. Each year he grew good turnips, but this year he was especially proud of one very big turnip. He left it in the ground longer than the others and watched with amazement and delight as it grew bigger and bigger. It grew so big that no one could remember ever having seen such a huge turnip before.

At last the old man decided that the time had come to pull it up. He took hold of the leaves of the great big turnip and pulled and pulled, but the turnip did not move.

So the old man called his wife to come and help. The old woman took hold of the old man, and the old man took hold of the turnip. Together they pulled and pulled, but still the turnip did not move.

So the old woman called her granddaughter to come and help. The granddaughter took hold of the old woman, the old woman took hold of the old man, and the old man took hold of the turnip. They pulled and pulled, but still the turnip did not move.

The granddaughter called to the dog to come and help. The dog took hold of the granddaughter, the granddaughter took hold of the old woman, the old woman took hold of the old man, and the old man took hold of the turnip. They pulled and pulled, but still the turnip did not move.

The dog called to the cat to come and help pull up the turnip. The cat took hold of the dog, the dog took hold of the grand-daughter, the granddaughter took hold of the old woman, the old woman took hold of the old man, and the old man took hold of

the turnip. They all pulled and pulled as hard as they could, but still the turnip did not move.

Then the cat called to a mouse to come and help pull up the great big turnip. The mouse took hold of the cat, the cat took hold of the dog, the dog took hold of the granddaughter, the grand-daughter took hold of the old woman, the old woman took hold of the old man, and he took hold of the turnip. Together they pulled and pulled and pulled as hard as they could.

Suddenly, the great big turnip came out of the ground, and everyone fell over.

The old woman chopped up the great big turnip and made a great big pot of delicious turnip soup. There was enough soup for everybody – the mouse, the cat, the dog, the granddaughter, the old woman and the old man. There was even some left over.

Rapunzel

A long time ago, a husband and wife lived happily in a cottage at the edge of a wood. But one day the wife fell ill. She could eat nothing and grew thinner and thinner. The only thing that could cure her, she believed, was a strange herb that grew in the beautiful garden next to their cottage. She begged her husband to find a way into the garden and steal some of this herb, which was called rapunzel.

Now this garden belonged to a wicked witch, who used it to grow herbs for her spells. One day, she caught the husband creeping into her garden. When he told her what he had come for, the witch gave him some rapunzel, but she made him promise to give her their firstborn child in return. The husband agreed, thinking that the witch would soon forget the promise. He took the

rapunzel back to the cottage and gave it to his wife. As soon as she had eaten it she felt better.

A year later, a baby girl was born and the witch *did* come and take her away. She told the couple they would be able to see their daughter in the garden behind their house. Over the years they were able to watch her grow up into a beautiful child, with long fair hair. The witch called her Rapunzel after the plant her father had come to take.

When she was twelve years old, the witch decided to lock Rapunzel up in a high tower in case she tried to run away. The tower had no door or staircase, but Rapunzel was quite happy up there as she could sit at the window watching the life of the forest and talking to the birds. Yet sometimes she would sigh, for she longed to be back in the beautiful garden where she could play in the sunshine. Then she would sing to cheer herself up.

Each day, the witch came to see her, bringing her fresh food. She would stand at the bottom of the tower and call out,

"Rapunzel, Rapunzel, let down your long hair."

Rapunzel, whose long golden hair was plaited, would twist it around one of the bars and drop it out of the window, and the witch would climb up it. When she left, Rapunzel would let down her golden hair again, and the witch would slide nimbly down.

One day, the king's son was riding through the forest when he heard Rapunzel singing. Mystified, he rode to the tower, but could see no door, so could not understand how anyone could be there. He decided to stay and watch the tower and listen to the singing. After a while the witch came along and the prince watched her carefully as she stood at the bottom of the tower and called out,

"Rapunzel, Rapunzel, let down your long hair."

To the prince's amazement, a long golden plait of hair fell almost to the ground. When he saw the witch climb up the hair and disappear through the window, he made up his mind he would wait until she had gone and see if he could do the same.

So after the witch had gone, he stood where the witch had been and called,

"Rapunzel, Rapunzel, let down your long hair."

When the golden plait came tumbling down, he climbed up as the witch had done and found to his astonishment the most beautiful girl he had ever seen. They talked for a long time and then the prince left, promising to come again. Rapunzel looked forward to his visits, for she had been lonely. He told her all about the world outside her tower, and they fell deeply in love.

One day Rapunzel said to the witch, "Why is it when you climb up my hair you are so heavy? The handsome prince who comes is much lighter than you." At this, the witch flew into a rage. She took Rapunzel out of the tower and led her deep into the forest

to a lonely spot, and told her she must stay there without food or shelter. The witch cut off Rapunzel's long plait of golden hair and then hurried back to the tower.

That evening when the prince came by, he called out as usual,

"Rapunzel, Rapunzel, let down your long hair."

The witch, who had fastened the plait of golden hair inside the window, threw it down. The prince climbed up eagerly, only to be confronted with the wicked witch. "Aha," she cackled, "so you are the visitor who has been coming to see my little Rapunzel. I will make sure you won't ever see her again," and she tried to scratch out his eyes.

The prince jumped out of the high window and landed in a clump of thorny bushes. His face, however, was badly scratched and his eyes hurt so much that he could not see, and he stumbled off blindly into the forest.

After several days of wandering and suffering, he heard somebody singing. Following the sound, he drew closer and realized he had found Rapunzel, who was singing as she worked to make a home for herself in the forest. He ran toward her, calling her name, and she came and kissed him. As she did so, his eyes were healed and he could see again.

The prince took Rapunzel to his father's palace, where he told their story. She was reunited with her parents, and then a grand wedding took place. Rapunzel married the prince and lived with him happily for many years. As for the witch, a royal proclamation banished her from the kingdom and she was never seen again.